MANNERS ARE MAGIC

"You'll Thank Me For Telling You"
Lessons on Life from Ms. Manners

Jean Abrahamson

D1016523

No Manners, No Life

No Manners, No Job

No Manners, No Happiness

For further information, contact the publisher at

Emmis Books
1700 Madison Road
Cincinnati, OH 45206
www.emmisbooks.com

Library of Congress Cataloging-in-Publication Data

Abrahamson, Jean
Manners are magic : "you'll thank me for telling you" lessons on life from
Ms. Manners / by Jean Abrahamson.
     p. cm.
  ISBN 1–57860–231–9
  1. Etiquette for children and teenagers. I. Title.
  BJ1631.A4 2005
  395.1'22--dc22
                          2005001584

Designed and Illustrated by Adam Greber
Edited by Stephanie VandeHaar

For my parents, who helped me know the importance of manners; and for my wonderful brother and sister, renowned ophthalmologists, who inspired me with their accomplishments. This is for all children and adults everywhere.

CONTENTS

Hometown Hero   1

Meeting and Greeting   2

Straight and Strong   4

Smile and Be Happy   6

Personality   8

Feelings   10

Listen and Learn from All Around You   12

Equal, but Different   14

No Fighting   16

Getting Along with Others   18

Attracting Attention the Wrong Way   20

Strive to Improve Yourself   22

Grammar   24

Going to School   26

Stay Healthy   28

Ladies and Gentleman   30

Restaurant and Table Manners   32

Museum Manners   34

Bathroom Manners   36

Telephone Manners   38

Thank You   40

And Lastly...   42

Author's Note   44

Hometown Hero

Ms. Jean Abrahamson, a Cincinnati native, has been a substitute teacher in the Cincinnati Public Schools for more than forty years. During that time, she has noticed that many young people do not exhibit the manners that many adults learned from their parents and others when they were children.

Ms. Abrahamson, our Ms. Manners, feels strongly about a young person's need to learn and employ proper manners. Dozens of times during her teaching career, she has used her own money to offer rewards for students who exhibit good behavior. This book is Ms. Manners' attempt to pass these manners onto those young people who were never taught, to those who may have forgotten, and to those who need a refresher course.

–William A. Weathers, *The Cincinnati Enquirer*

MEETING AND GREETING

When you meet someone, you should extend your right hand in greeting. Always press a person's hand firmly to show you have a warm feeling toward him or her. Never give a "weak fish" handshake. A firm handshake shows confidence.

Remember to stand up when meeting someone. It shows respect for this person. Having respect for others is one of the keys of good manners.

The best way to meet a new friend or to get a good job is to look someone in the eye. This shows that you are interested in what he or she is saying. Everybody likes a good listener. This is especially important if you are trying to get a job because it shows that you are willing to listen and learn. If you look down at the floor, you may appear shy or dishonest because you don't look another person in the eye.

It is important to be on time! Be punctual. If you can't make an appointment or meeting, call ahead and let someone know. Other people's time is just as important as your own, so don't keep people waiting for you.

STRAIGHT AND STRONG

Good posture is important. If you sit up and stand up straight, you look important. Your clothes look better. A straight back is important to good looks. When you stand up straight and have good posture, you appear confident and important.

Sit straight. Stand straight. Walk straight. When you are young, your backbone is forming, and having good posture helps make you strong.

People can form an opinion of you right away just by the way you carry yourself. Older people also appear younger simply with a straight back. If you walk hunched over, you may look tired or stressed, worried or unsure of yourself, even if you are not.

You look your very best if you walk with a straight back.

SMILE AND BE HAPPY

Always look on the bright side of life. If you laugh, you last. Always have a sense of humor! Being able to laugh and be happy no matter what happens is one of the keys to having a good life. Don't take annoying things or people too seriously. Things you may worry about will pass, and your worry will be forgotten if you can always smile and be happy.

Everybody likes to be around happy people at school, work, and at home.

You can't have a healthy body unless you have a happy mind, and you can't have a happy mind unless you have a healthy body.

A smile shows friendship all over the world. Everyone deserves to be greeted with a smile. A smile is an inexpensive way to improve your looks. Don't walk around with a frown or an angry look on your face. Everyone has troubles that can make them look unhappy. But if you act happy and keep busy, sooner or later, you'll feel happy, too. Your feelings show on your face. No one likes being around a sourpuss. Most people like to be around cheerful, smiling people. If you're unhappy, it shows. If you're sad, it shows. If you're grumpy, it shows. Did you know that unhappiness can upset your stomach, make you lose your appetite, keep you from a good night's sleep, and even give you an itch without a rash?

So smile and make someone else smile. Smile and the world smiles with you.

PERSONALITY

Reading books, magazines, and newspapers helps expand your mind and develop your very own personality. If you listen to the news or take trips to interesting places, you'll have lots to talk about and will learn how to carry on a conversation with anyone.

It's fun to find out things about other people. Finding out what people think about or like to do helps you learn and develop a good personality and mind. Ask good questions and then listen and learn.

No one is born knowing how to do things the right way. Life is a marvelous challenge. You learn to walk, talk, catch, jump, ride, and skate. You can take lessons or learn from books. You can learn how to swim, play tennis, play golf, ride a bike, or jump rope. Participating in sports, whether you watch or play, can help you get to know many new people and make new friends.

For some people, it can take several years to learn to play tennis, golf, baseball, football, or basketball. But once you learn a new skill, it's yours forever. If you do something well, people will respect you.

You are special! No one is any better than you. However, the only thing that makes you appear better is a good education and good manners. These are a big part of your personality.

If you respect and like yourself, other people will respect and like you. Having good manners means having integrity and honesty.

Integrity is something you develop inside your heart. Be honest with yourself first. Having integrity means that you don't cheat and you always do your best. Be a good sport and congratulate your opponent, even if you lose. Never "boo" anyone. The good that you do with your life is what will be remembered.

FEELINGS

We all have feelings. Treat people the way you would like them to treat you or your family. Hold your head high.

Don't say mean things to people. Don't gossip. Think before you talk. Sass is not class! Class means having good manners. Do not sass your parents, teachers, grandparents, or other adults. If you can't say something nice, don't say anything at all. It's better to give a compliment to someone than an insult.

Being kind is more important than being right. Be considerate of other people's feelings.

When you feel sad or unhappy, think of someone else and do something nice for that person. Doing things for other people makes you feel better! Many people are worse off than you, both mentally and physically. Think of others who are less fortunate and your troubles will seem minor.

Never feel sorry for yourself. Feeling sorry for yourself is the worst sickness there is. Think, mind over matter! If you don't mind, it won't matter. You can use your brain to overcome anything and accomplish whatever you want.

Don't carry a chip on your shoulder or bear a grudge. If you remember the good things in life and forget the negative ones, you'll be happier. You can only hurt yourself, so don't make yourself miserable.

Loving yourself and others is very important. It doesn't matter how old or young you are; you can have and give love at any age.

LISTEN AND LEARN FROM ALL AROUND YOU

Always remember the three "R's." Show Respect. Be Responsible. Be Reliable. Respect others, be responsible for yourself and your actions, and be reliable. If you say you are going to do something, do it.

Learn to be a good listener. If you can look someone in the eye, it means you are honest and will never lie, steal, or cheat. If you listen to what people say, you are really interested in learning and don't already think of yourself as a "know-it-all."

I feel I can learn from everybody. I feel that we are all put on this earth to help others. I was fortunate to have wonderful parents who taught me values, self-esteem, and how to always do the right thing. They had many hobbies—playing music, sports, and cards—and were successful in all the things they tried.

You can learn to do anything you want. The world is open to you if you learn to listen to it.

EQUAL, BUT DIFFERENT

God created all of us. No one is better than anyone else. Two things that help set you apart are having good manners and a good education.

I call my body my machine. We may look different, but we are all the same inside our machine. Never make fun of how someone looks. Don't tease or make fun of people who aren't like you.

Some people are born with healthier machines than others. Unfortunately, some people are born blind, deaf, minus a finger or toe, or have other physical disabilities. But sometimes they accomplish more in life than those with no disabilities (like the famous composer, Beethoven, who became deaf). They go through life just like people who are not physically challenged.

Some people talk loudly because they can't hear very well. Some people have difficulty pronouncing words (for example, saying "wake" when trying to say "lake"). Don't tease or make fun of them. Remember everyone wants to share his or her feelings and thoughts.

Don't tease or make fun of someone because he or she doesn't have the newest style of clothes or sneakers. (As long as a person's clothes are neat and clean, he or she should be treated with respect.)

Don't dislike or judge people just because they are a different color or follow a different religion. This is called having prejudices. It's never too late to change your mind about people or give up prejudices about races or religion. Have tolerance for everyone around you, even if you disagree about religion or politics. Always be polite and tolerant. Treat everyone as you wish to be treated.

No Fighting

Remember it takes two to argue or fight. Maybe someone doesn't feel well, so whatever he or she has to do becomes harder. People can become irritable or cranky. We all have moods. When you respect someone, you understand his or her feelings. Our loved ones put up with our moods, so we can put up with theirs.

However, when a stranger calls you an ugly name or tries to start a fight, *be smart.* Click off your ear as if you didn't hear or turn your head as if you can't see. In other words, *ignore* the person. Or you can look the person in the face and *smile* to show that what was said didn't bother you.

It takes two to fight and argue. You shouldn't be a "copycat"—don't copy and get mad. Simply walk away. And if you don't pay attention to the person, a fight can be avoided. This can hurt more than a punch or a kick. You're using psychology (your brain) to outwit someone. Two wrongs don't make a right.

Avoid bullies. Rather than confront them, inform your teacher or an adult about their actions.

Don't have a "short fuse" and get angry easily. Don't hit back. Don't throw things. Don't yell back. Learn to stay calm and avoid fights or arguments. Count to ten or take deep breaths so you don't lose your temper. Remember this all your life and you'll have a happy house!

GETTING ALONG WITH OTHERS

Learn to get along with others. We're all the same inside. All of us want happiness, good health, and to get the best out of life.

Don't shout or say "shut up." Talk or discuss quietly. This is good manners.

It isn't right or normal to throw a tantrum and yell to get what you want. Talk things over in a normal voice and discuss what bothers you. Treat others the way you would like to be treated. Don't say things to hurt family or friends. I don't like to be around people who are always putting other people down.

You'll never be sorry for things you haven't said. If you say something hurtful, you can never take it back despite saying, "I'm sorry."

People who try to start fights or arguments are not going to be with you for the rest of your life. *You* are going to be with yourself. If you let someone upset you and you lose your temper, then you are not in control of yourself. We are responsible for how we feel.

Learn to use self-control. Think before you do something bad. Afterward, you might be punished or your conscience will bother you. You have to live with yourself. Learn by other people's mistakes.

Stay away from bad people. Choose your friends. To have a friend, be a friend. Live and play around good people.

ATTRACTING ATTENTION THE WRONG WAY

When you are loud and obnoxious, you are seeking attention. Some kids "show off" and disturb the classroom. They don't have good manners.

Unhappy people try to make other people unhappy. They are usually the ones who fight, argue, sass, and try to get others in trouble. They will do anything to try and make others notice them—throw crayons, break pencils, sneak out of the room, and generally act dumb and unruly. Don't let an unhappy person pull you down!

Never be loud or use profanity! Don't litter or leave trash anywhere. Put all your trash in a trashcan. Don't leave your shopping cart out in the middle of the parking lot. Take a minute to take it back to the store or put it in the round-up rack.

If you want attention and respect, do something well and others will look up to you. You can also earn respect by being kind and nice to others and helping the less fortunate.

STRIVE TO IMPROVE YOURSELF

Read a lot—both books and newspapers. Use good grammar. Use a wide-ranging vocabulary to express your thoughts. Listen to the news.

If you have good manners, keep busy, and find work that you love, you'll enjoy life. Take pride in your work. Always strive to do your best!

Attitude is so important. If you decide the work you do in school or at home is fun, it will be—whether it's washing the dishes, washing the car, scrubbing floors, raking leaves, shoveling snow, or doing school work. All these tasks can be fun if you let them, and then you will feel like you've accomplished something.

Don't procrastinate—this means putting off or ignoring things that you should be doing or starting. Don't let time get away from you just because you feel lazy or unsure. Just begin what you have to do and don't worry about when you'll finish. The important thing is simply to start.

Be adventurous and don't be afraid to try new and different things. Learn how to do as many different things as you can. You never know when you are going to need to take care of yourself or someone else.

If people are good, we'll have a good world. Never do anything you'll be ashamed of or that will make others ashamed to be with you. Life is what you make it. You can be anyone you want to be on earth! If you have a goal and go after what you want, you can achieve anything.

GRAMMAR

It's fun to use the dictionary to learn new words. Look up words you don't know to improve your vocabulary. Use these new words as much as you can. Using the dictionary will help you have a good vocabulary and become more intelligent.

Learn to pronounce words correctly. Don't slur your words or use slang. If you speak properly, you show you are smart. For instance, don't pronounce the word "truth" by saying "troof." Don't say "dis" when you mean "this." Using slang or trying to sound like everyone else doesn't make you sound cool; it only makes you sound uneducated or dumb.

Learn the proper uses of the verb "to be." Say "I am," "she is," or "they are." Don't use "ain't." Never say, "you is" or "you was." The proper form is either "you are" or "you were."

If you point at something, don't say "them are mine." Instead say, "those are mine."

Speaking correctly and knowing proper grammar and pronunciation is one of the most important things you can learn. It is important to learn to speak and write correctly in order to communicate with others.

GOING TO SCHOOL

Open and close your desk quietly. Be happy that you are able to go to school. Everyone is there for the same reason as you—to learn many wonderful things. So don't waste your time. You cannot get a good job without a good education!

Wait your turn getting on the bus. Cooperate with the driver. Stay quiet—having good bus manners means no fighting, loud talking, or cursing.

Listen to your teacher, who works hard to present new ideas to you. Your teacher cannot teach you if you don't listen. Everyone in the class hears the same explanation from your teacher at the same time. So you must concentrate. This means shutting out all other thoughts except what you are hearing or doing at that time. And if you don't understand something, talk to your teacher about it. Your teacher will appreciate that you are trying and will offer extra help. Your teacher may also have someone else help you, like one of your classmates.

Keep your desk neat and in order. This will help keep your studies and homework in order, and helps you keep your life in order.

An education is important, so never stop learning!

STAY HEALTHY

If you haven't eaten properly or gotten enough rest, you'll be too tired to learn your lessons or play with other students. You can't go to school to learn or enjoy playing if you don't feel well.

If you don't get enough sleep, you may have trouble thinking clearly. Everyone needs eight to ten hours of sleep.

Exercise is important! I call my body "my machine." I work with a trainer twice a week to keep my machine in shape and healthy.

If I don't put gas in my car, it won't go. If I don't put water in my body, it also will not go. My machine needs six to eight glasses of water every day. I don't mean coke or soda! I mean water. Water helps you digest food, helps your plumbing system work properly, and keeps the body at the right temperature—98.6 degrees.

Don't smoke cigarettes. They are bad for your health. Cigarettes are addictive. If you don't start smoking, you'll never have to worry about trying to stop. Don't drink alcohol or do drugs! Drugs can ruin you, your future, and your family.

Eat properly. Eating healthy food, especially for breakfast, makes it easier to learn. Breakfast is the most important meal of the day. Eating a good breakfast helps you have enough energy for the rest of the day, stimulates your brain, and gives energy to your muscles.

Everyone needs a balanced diet. You should eat three meals a day. Try to eat five servings of fruits or vegetables everyday. If you need a snack between meals, eat an apple or some nuts. Don't eat candy or cookies! All your meals should be healthy, with a good balance of protein (like meat and fish), dairy products, breads, fruits, and vegetables. The right combination of all these foods helps keep your diet balanced and your body healthy.

LADIES AND GENTLEMEN

A girl is a lady. She is soft-spoken, kind, thoughtful, and considerate to others. A lady is someone who is educated, speaks with good grammar, and never stops learning new things. A lady makes a happy home for herself and her family.

A boy is a gentleman. He is gentle and kind, shows respect, likes to work, and speaks with good grammar. A gentleman never hits a woman, child, or baby, and never demeans or belittles another person. A gentleman removes his hat when he enters a home, when a woman gets on an elevator, and when he's introduced to someone. He stands up when someone older enters the room, when people come by his table to say hello in a restaurant, and when the lady leaves the table to go to the powder room. He stands again when she returns to the dinner table. A gentleman stands behind a lady's chair and slides it in toward the table as she sits down.

A gentleman opens the door for a lady. A gentleman opens and closes a car door for a lady. If dining with a lady, a gentleman asks the lady what she would like to have after they both have had time to look at the menu.

Ladies and gentlemen wait their turns in lines. They don't push ahead of other people or make a scene if they have to wait. Have patience. Patience is a virtue.

When you visit people in their homes, do not put your coat on the floor or your feet on any of the furniture. It's thoughtful to bring a gift when visiting, such as candy, flowers, or baked goods.

Gentlemen and ladies always display their good manners. You should frequently use good manners words such as "please," "excuse me" or "pardon me," "thank you," and "you're welcome."

RESTAURANT
AND TABLE MANNERS

When you are seated at a table, take the napkin and put it on your lap. A napkin on your lap helps keep your clothes clean, and is the place to wipe your sticky fingers and your mouth. If there are more than two people at the table, be sure to participate in the conversation. Don't sit there like a bump on a log. Have something interesting to talk about. Get people to converse. Ask questions and be a good listener.

Don't use a toothpick at the dinner table. Don't stretch while at the table. If you have to yawn, cover your mouth!

Turn your head and cover your mouth and nose when you sneeze or cough. Don't use a napkin as a handkerchief. Always keep your elbows off the table. Never talk while you have food in your mouth. This is both rude and unattractive. In the same way, always chew your food with your mouth closed. Chewing with your mouth open sounds and looks gross.

Don't reach across the table for anything. Politely ask someone to pass you the item you need. Take only small amounts; you can always have more later.

Be aware of proper table settings. The forks and napkin are always placed to the left of the dinner plate. The knives and spoons are placed on the right, with the knives closest to the plate. The salad plate is placed to the left of the forks. If there are two forks, the smaller one is for the salad. A small bread or butter plate is placed above the forks. After cutting your meat, lay your knife across the upper edge of the dinner plate.

The drinking glasses are placed above the knives and spoons. The coffee or tea cup is placed to the right of the spoons. If there are two spoons, the one with the larger bowl is the soup spoon and the smaller one is the tea spoon. Remember, you use the tea spoon to stir your coffee or tea so leave the spoon on the cup's saucer plate.

The table is cleared before dessert is served. If you are a guest, you can offer to help clear the table.

MUSEUM MANNERS

Whenever you are fortunate enough to visit a museum, always remember that the art and treasures inside are for everyone to appreciate and enjoy for many years to come.

Remember these important points:

(1) Look, study, and enjoy the composition, colors, and subject matter. You can learn how people looked, dressed, or lived in the past from a painting.

(2) Read the artist's name, the year he or she was born, and the medium that he or she used—oil, water color, pastels, or ink. Then look and enjoy. You will soon learn to recognize the artist's style.

(3) Never touch a painting; you could damage it.

(4) Don't run or play in a museum.

(5) Throw litter in a trash can.

(6) And most important, remember that a great work of art can be enjoyed forever.

Many people like to surround themselves with art, sometimes with copies or the originals. An original is a single work produced by the artist, and can be very expensive. However, art can be an investment and gain in value as time goes by. It's fun to find out about an artist's life and learn about his or her style.

BATHROOM MANNERS

Remember that someone else will be using the bathroom after you leave. Try to leave the bathroom as clean and neat as you found it (or cleaner!). Remember to flush the toilet.

When you are finished, always put the lid down. Both ladies and gentlemen cover the seat with the lid before leaving. This is both good manners and safety conscious. A small child or pet could play in the toilet if the lid is left open. A child or animal could fall in, get hurt, or even drown.

Always remember to wash your hands. After you wash your hands, throw the used paper towels in the trash can (not on the floor). If you splatter soap or water on the sink, wipe it clean before you leave.

If you have used the last of the toilet paper, replace it with a new roll. After you have taken a bath, be sure to clean the bathtub so it's ready for the next person who uses it. Don't leave dirty towels or washcloths on the floor or sink. Put used items in the dirty-clothes hamper or hang them on a rack.

Telephone Manners

Always answer the phone with a pleasant "Hello!"
If you answer the phone and it is for you, you should say,
"This is he," or "This is she," not "This is me," "This is
him," or "This is her." Always start with asking the person
on the other line, "How are you?"

If you recognize the person calling you, sound happy
that he or she called you. Say, "It's nice to hear from you!"

When you hang up, always say, "Thanks for calling!"
and, "It was good to talk to you, and I hope to see you soon."
If you have a cell phone, don't use it where it could bother
other people, such as in restaurants, movie theaters, crowded
buses, or stores. It is rude and distracting to talk loudly on
the phone and intrude on other people's privacy. Don't make
people wait to talk to you because you're busy talking on
your cell phone. This is very rude. Most important, do not
use your cell phone if you are driving. It's very dangerous
to talk on the phone instead of concentrating on traffic,
conditions, and driving the car.

THANK YOU

Always remember to say "thank you!"

Say thank you when someone hands you something. Say thank you when someone holds the door for you. Say thank you when someone holds the elevator for you. Say thank you when someone runs an errand for you. Say thank you when someone gives you a gift. Say thank you when someone passes food to you at the table, or when someone treats you to a meal or beverage. Say thanks when someone helps you fix something, and when someone does you a favor. Say thank you when someone helps you pick up something that you have dropped.

When appropriate, thank-you notes are a great way to say thank you!

Say thank you when someone compliments you on your appearance, your good grades, or your good manners. It's nice to compliment others.

Always saying thank you is having good manners. And manners are magic!

And Lastly...

In 2004, a terrible earthquake erupted in the ocean off the coast of south Asia and caused a terrible tsunami (a huge and destructive wave of water). Without warning, more than 167,000 people lost their lives and homes. The devastation was unbelievable, and the entire world grieved.

In 2001, another disaster occurred in America when four planes were crashed into the World Trade Center, the Pentagon, and a field in Pennsylvania. Again, the number of lives lost and lives changed was unbelievable, and the whole world was shaken by this tragedy.

My final message to you is important: Make something with your life while you are here! Life is short, and you never know when unexpected events will make permanent changes. Live each day to its fullest. You should get a good education and a job you'll enjoy, and work to help others along the way.

Don't waste your time with silly fighting, pushing, or doing things that hurt yourself and others. Attitude is everything, so use good sense in all that you do and commit your heart to.

Remember how lucky you really are. Appreciate what you have and you can do anything you want to do. Life is fragile, so handle it prayerfully and with good manners!

This is my legacy to you.

IF I HAD MY CHILD TO RAISE OVER AGAIN
by *Diana Loomans*

If I had my child to raise all over again,
I'd finger paint more, and point the finger less.
I'd do less correcting, and more connecting.
I'd take my eyes off my watch, and watch with my eyes.
I would care to know less, and know to care more.
I'd take more hikes and fly more kites.
I'd stop playing serious, and seriously play.
I'd run through more fields, and gaze at more stars.
I'd do more hugging, and less tugging.
I would be firm less often, and affirm much more.
I'd build self-esteem first, and the house later.
I'd teach less about the love of power,
And more about the power of love.

Author's Note

I have been very fortunate in my life to have met people from all over the world and from all walks of life. One of the many things that has impressed me is the different ways in which people approach life and their fellow man. I have been a school teacher for more than forty years and have encountered children from many different environments and family backgrounds. It is my assessment that many of them have not been educated in the proper relationships with their fellow human beings, older or younger, brothers or sisters, parents or relatives, teachers or strangers. They lack proper manners.

I want to help this world. By taking the time to teach manners, I am trying to enrich the lives of children by motivating them to enjoy reading, art, music, and crafts. I am hoping that with a little help, they'll be able to enrich their lives and the lives of their own children. Manners are magic!

DATE DUE
